I0173030

Worry Shy

A Story to Help Children Better Understand and Manage Social Anxiety

Little C Books

Corbett Shwom

Copyright © 2023 Corbett Shwom.

ISBN-13: 979-8-218-31262-6

All rights reserved. This book or any portion thereof may not be reproduced or used in any manner whatsoever without the express written permission of the author except for the use of brief quotations in a book review.

The contents of this book is not an attempt to practice medicine or give specific medical advice concerning mental health. The book is intended to be informational and a motivational tool that may help the reader with their Social Anxiety. It is not intended to be a substitute for professional advice, diagnosis, or treatment. Always seek the advice of a mental health professional or other qualified health provider with any questions you may have regarding Social Anxiety.

Published by Worry House Press.
First Edition
Printed in the United States of America.

www.corbettshwom.com

You see, Little C felt uneasy each day,
nervous and uncertain in every way.

He would make an excuse, or put on a spin,
anything to avoid a social situation.

He would dread for days and weeks ahead,
and would rather stay at home instead.

His mind raced, always feeling judged,
lost in his thoughts that endlessly nudged.

Who will be there? I don't know.
I so don't want to go.

Will I be asked a question?
Will I sound dumb?
Will I trip over my tongue?

Will I get upset if
I start to sweat?

If I stand alone to
avoid the mob,
will that make me
look like a snob?

Will I have to eat?
Will I sit in the right seat?

Will there be a crowd?
Will they think I'm chewing too loud?

My heart
will be racing.

My mouth
will be dry.

I'll feel like
I want to cry.

I'll just want to get out of there
to get a breath of fresh air.

And at the end of every day,
it would be the day on replay.

S-ST-S

Little C's thoughts would overflow,
questioning all he'd come to know.

All these thoughts in my mind,
how they constantly weigh.
How I so wish they would go away.

So one day, Little C, being as brave as he could be, asked his mother,

"Why do I care so much about what others think of me and what they might say? It's a constant worry every day."

"I don't know why, dear," she said.

"But we should go ask your doctor instead.
Thank you for having the courage to let
me know. Now, off to the doctor we go."

What a surprise to Little C when it came to be that he had something called **social anxiety**.

His doctor said, "To simplify, you're **worry shy**. It starts with a worry about what others might say, thinking they're judging you as you go through the day.

"You find it hard to speak up or join in the fun, feeling like you want to hide or just want to run.

"So you begin to doubt yourself and feel very small, thinking you're not good enough, not worthy at all.

"And because of all this worry about how others will perceive you, you start to avoid, or stop doing the things you like to do.

"And the nerves, the racing heart, the palms getting sweaty, they're all part of a natural response to get you ready, to get you steady.

"When we encounter what seems like danger or fear, our body kicks into gear, and these feelings appear.

"In our minds, our thoughts may grow big and strong. But remember, not all worries are where we belong. Most are just illusions, not really what's going on."

With the help of his doctor and support from his parents, Little C started to face social anxiety's fray by using the coping strategies he learned to help navigate each day.

SOCIAL ANXIETY TOOLKIT

Take deep breaths,
let worries go,
inhale bravery,
let your confidence show.

Visualize success,
see it in your
mind.

Trust in yourself,
leave your
fears behind.

Challenge negative thoughts,
let positive ones shine through.

BELIEVE
IN
YOURSELF

Believe in yourself,
there's nothing you can't do.

Start small, take a breath,
and face your fear.

With each new
experience, your
courage will appear.

Practice makes perfect, as the saying goes. With each exposure, your confidence will steadily grow.

With a trusted friend or family member,
pretend and play.
Practice social skills every day.

And remember to celebrate your wins,
big and small.

Cheer for yourself and stand tall.

And with time and practice,
Little C found his way.

In social situations, he
felt more at play.

He learned that everyone feels fear and stress,
but being himself was the way to impress.

He faced his fears with all his might,
showing his true self, shining bright.

He also knew it was okay to feel a little scared,
but he didn't let it stop him,
because he was now brave and prepared.

Author's Note

Embrace your uniqueness, you're one of a kind.
Don't let social anxiety take over your mind.

Remember, you're strong and brave. Let
that shine through. With self-acceptance,
you'll find your breakthrough.

With the brave steps you take, one by one, I know you'll
conquer social anxiety and get back to having fun.

How do I know? Well, you see, Little C was me.

Other Titles By
Corbett Shwom

Worry Habits

A Story to Help Children Better
Understand and Manage OCD

Worry Thoughts

A Story to Help Children Manage
Worries and Anxious Thoughts

Newsletter

Get notified about Little C updates
and new book releases.

corbettshwom.com

www.ingramcontent.com/pod-product-compliance
Lightning Source LLC
Chambersburg PA
CBHW072039060426
42449CB00010BA/2355